Dragon Tales

IN THE MUSHROOM MEADOW

I wish, I wish
With all my heart
To fly with dragons
In a land apart.

By Alison Inches

Illustrated by The Thompson Brothers

Based on the characters by Ron Rodecker

Visit Dragon Tales on the Web at www.dragontales.com

Watch us on PBS!

Max stood on tiptoe in front of the growth chart on the playroom wall. "Do you think I'm big enough to ride the bumper cars this year?" he asked his sister, Emmy.

Emmy measured Max. He hadn't grown at all.

"Maybe not this year," said Emmy.

Max groaned. "I'm tired of being little! I can't even reach the water fountain at school," he complained.

"Maybe the dragons can help with your little problem. Get it? 'Little' problem?" Emmy laughed.

Max's face brightened. The children grabbed their magic dragon scale.

Then they said the magic dragon poem,
    "*I wish, I wish*
    With all my heart
    To fly with dragons
    In a land apart."
    Whoosh! A circle of sparkles swirled them away
to Dragon Land.

Max and Emmy played kickball while they waited for their dragon friends to finish flying practice.

"Watch how high I can make it go!" cried Emmy. She kicked the ball way over Max's head, and it landed—*plop!*—right in the middle of Mushroom Meadow.

"I'll get it!" they both shouted as they ran after the ball. They raced into the meadow and brushed past two violets that had just opened their petals. *Poof!* The startled violets showered the children with magical sparkles.

"Uh-oh!" said Max.
"We're shrinking!" gasped Emmy.
They got smaller and smaller until they
were no taller than a blade of grass.

"We're sorry!" said one of the flowers. "We're shrinking violets. When we bloom, everything that touches us shrinks!"

"This could be fun for a while," Max said, looking at the giant flowers. "You can *un*-shrink us later."

"I wish we could," said the violet. "But we don't know how."

"You mean I'll be small forever?" Max cried. "Now I'll *never* get to ride the bumper cars!"

Max and Emmy could hear the dragons, high above Mushroom Meadow, calling their names.

"Down here!" cried the children. "Down here!"

But it was no use. The dragons couldn't hear them.

"I wish we could just go home," said Max.

"Oh, come on, Max," said Emmy. "Let's try to figure this out. At first you said being shrunk would be fun. I bet we can think of a way to let the dragons know we're here."

Max and Emmy looked around the meadow. A crowd of caterpoozles, snails, toads, turtles, and bugs had gathered around them. Emmy knocked politely on a turtle's shell until he poked out his head.

"Would you give us a ride back to our dragon friends?" she asked.

"Climb aboard!" said the turtle.

Even though the turtle was big, he moved very slowly. "I ca-a-an't he-e-elp be-e-eing sssslllo-o-oww," said the turtle. "I-i-it's ju-u-ust my-y-yy wa-a-ay."

"It's very nice of you to give us a lift," said Max. "But this could take *forever.*"

Next, Max waved at a dragonfly flying by.
"Would you fly us to our friends?" asked Max.
The dragonfly agreed, so Max and Emmy
climbed onto her back.

"Ready for liftoff!" shouted Max.

"*Urr-umph!*" said the dragonfly, frantically flapping her wings. "*Urr-umph!*" Even though she was the biggest bug in the meadow, she could not lift them.

"Abort mission," said Max sadly. "I guess I'm too big, even though I'm so little."

"If only we were bigger," said Max. "Then our friends could see us."

"Wait! I just thought of a way to make us look bigger," said Emmy. "We can make a pyramid! If we climb on each other's backs, the dragons will be able to see us!"

The bugs and critters were happy to help and formed a magnificent pyramid. But when Max and Emmy climbed on top, the pyramid began to sway. It swayed to one side and then the other. Then—*crash!* Everyone tumbled to the ground.

Max landed in the path of some busy ants.
"Need some help?" asked one of the ants.
"You're too little," said Max. "How could *you* help us?"
"We can lift *very* heavy things," said the ant proudly.
"So?" said Max. "Anyone can do . . . Whoa! You weren't kidding!"

"Have you got an idea how we can make our friends notice us?" asked Emmy.

"We'll build you a ramp so you can climb on top of the tallest mushroom," the ant said enthusiastically. "Then you can bounce high into the air until your friends can see you."

"Cool!" Max shouted.

The ants lifted some sticks and made a big ramp. Max and Emmy, as well as many of their new friends, climbed up the ramp and started hopping up and down on the bouncy mushroom cap.

Soon Ord spotted the tiny critters—and his friends Max and Emmy—bouncing high on the mushroom trampoline.

"There you are!" shouted Ord. "We knew you must have been shrunk when we found your ball next to the shrinking violets."

"Let's go see Quetzal," said Cassie. "He might be able to help Max and Emmy get back to their real size."

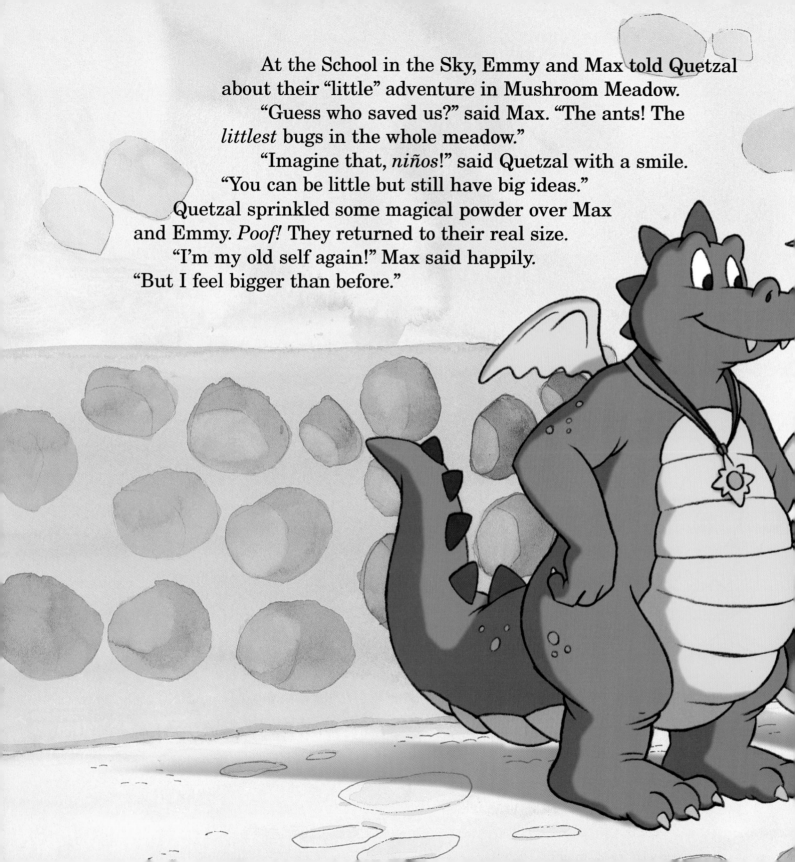

At the School in the Sky, Emmy and Max told Quetzal about their "little" adventure in Mushroom Meadow.

"Guess who saved us?" said Max. "The ants! The *littlest* bugs in the whole meadow."

"Imagine that, *niños!*" said Quetzal with a smile. "You can be little but still have big ideas."

Quetzal sprinkled some magical powder over Max and Emmy. *Poof!* They returned to their real size.

"I'm my old self again!" Max said happily. "But I feel bigger than before."

Back home in the playroom, Max decided to make his own bumper cars out of laundry baskets.

"I may not be big enough for the bumper cars at Funland," he said, "but I've got *big* ideas!"

"Way to go, Max!" cried Emmy as she gave him a high five.